Polly Bobblehop Makes a Mess

Daisy Meadows

ORCHARD

Can you keep a secret? I thought you could!

Then I'll tell you about an enchanted wood.

It lies through the door in the old oak tree,

Let's go there now - just follow me!

We'll find adventure that never ends,

And meet the Magic Animal Friends!

Love,
Goldie the Cat

Contents

CHAPTER ONE: A New Adventure   9

CHAPTER TWO: Friendship Forest in Danger!   23

CHAPTER THREE: Swept Away!   37

CHAPTER FOUR: Mr Stoutfoot's Wonderful Boots   49

CHAPTER FIVE: Boggit Swamp   61

CHAPTER SIX: Lovely Mud!   69

CHAPTER SEVEN: Bubbles and Burps!   79

CHAPTER EIGHT: Party at the Bobblehops'   93

CHAPTER ONE

A New Adventure

"This cake's going to be really yummy,"
said Lily Hart, stirring a creamy mixture
in a large bowl. "Vanilla sponge is Mum's
favourite – and she loves raspberry
filling."

Lily and her best friend Jess Forester
were in Jess's kitchen. They were making a

 9

surprise birthday cake for Lily's mother.

"Dad can put it in the oven for us when it's ready to bake," replied Jess.

"And we'll cover it in candles and sugar roses and give it to Mum when it's finished!" said Lily.

Jess and her dad lived in a cottage opposite Lily's house, where Mr and Mrs Hart ran the Helping Paw Wildlife Hospital. The two vets had set up the hospital in their garden and never turned a sick animal away. Lily and Jess loved helping with the little patients whenever they could.

"Miaow!"

Pixie, Jess's kitten, suddenly sprang on to
the counter The tiny tabby didn't see the
cake bowl. She skidded straight into the
side of the bowl and it tipped over! Batter
splattered all over the counter and all over
her fur – right to the white tip of her tail.

"What a mess!" gasped Jess as Pixie's
cheeky yellow eyes peeked out from
under the mixture. "But she looks so
funny!"

"And so adorable," giggled Lily.

Jess started wiping the mixture off Pixie
before the mischievous kitten could eat it.

 11

Pixie wriggled from her grasp and ran
to the window.

"What is it, Pixie?" asked Jess. She saw
something moving outside and gave a

gasp of delight. "Look, Lily!"

A beautiful golden-haired cat leapt on to the sill and pawed at the glass.

"Goldie!" exclaimed Lily.

"She must want us to go to Friendship Forest!" breathed Jess. She hung up her apron. "Come on!"

Whenever Goldie appeared, Lily and Jess knew they were going on a magical adventure. Friendship Forest was a secret place full of adorable little woodland creatures who lived in wonderful homes among the trees. And – best of all – they could talk!

"Wait," called Lily. "We can't leave the kitchen for your dad to clean."

"Don't forget, no time passes while we're in Friendship Forest," replied Jess, grinning. "We'll clear up when we get back."

Lily whipped off her own apron and dashed into the garden after Jess. The girls ran to greet their friend, but Goldie gave an urgent miaow and bounded away.

"Goldie seems worried," said Lily.

"Let's find out why," said Jess. She had a horrible feeling that something bad had happened in Friendship Forest.

They followed
Goldie through the
gate and down the
side of Lily's garden,
towards Brightley
Meadow. The girls
caught a glimpse of
the animal patients
in their pens as they
dashed past. A crow
with a healing wing
gave them a friendly
caw from the aviary.

They leapt across

the stream and into the meadow where
a huge old oak stood. The tree seemed
dead and forlorn, but as Goldie drew near
it came alive. Every branch burst with
bright, shiny leaves, goldfinches darted
among the branches and bumblebees
hummed around the pretty pink flowers
below.

Goldie touched the bark with her paw
and at once, two words became visible.
Quickly, Lily and Jess held hands and
read them aloud: "Friendship Forest!"

A door with a leaf-shaped handle
appeared in the trunk. It swung open and

warm yellow light spilled through.

Goldie hurried through the door.
As the girls stepped into the light, they
felt themselves shrink a little. The glow
faded and now they were standing in the
magical forest. Tiny, charming cottages
were dotted about in a sunlit clearing.
The air was full of enchanting birdsong
and a gentle breeze made the trees wave
merrily. Dandyroses sent out delicious
scents of strawberry milkshake.

Goldie was standing on her hind legs
and was almost as tall as the girls. She
wore a glittery scarf round her neck.

"Thank goodness you could come," she
said anxiously.

Lily and Jess ran to give her a big
hello hug. But instead of feeling the soft,
springy moss that usually covered the
ground, they splashed through muddy
puddles. Something was clearly very

wrong in Friendship Forest.

"Has Grizelda done this?" gasped Lily.

Grizelda was a wicked witch who wanted the animals to leave the forest so she could have it for herself. Lily and Jess often had to stop her carrying out her nasty schemes.

"Who else?" said a crackly voice.

The girls turned to see a greenish-yellow orb appear in the air. It burst, sending smelly sparks showering everywhere. In its place stood a tall, thin woman. She wore a purple tunic, tight black trousers and long boots with spiky

heels. Her scowling face peered out through greasy green hair. It was Grizelda!

"I might have known you pests would poke your noses in," she screeched at the girls. "Well, you're wasting your time. My wonderful plan cannot fail. Remember the Master Map of Friendship Forest?"

The magical Master Map showed everything in the whole of Friendship Forest. The map was divided into four parts, each looked after by a different

woodland family. If something changed
in the forest, the map changed. And if
anything changed on the map, the forest
changed too. First Grizelda had stolen the
map of the south and torn it, so a huge
chasm appeared in the ground. Then
she'd snatched the map of the north and
scribbled on it so everywhere was covered
in nasty thorns and vines. Lily and Jess had
foiled her both times.

"I've taken the map of the east from
the Bobblehop family," Grizelda went on.
She cackled with delight. "Ha! Those silly
wallabies couldn't do anything to stop me."

"You won't get away with this, Grizelda!" said Jess crossly.

"Yes I will," shrieked Grizelda. "Soon the forest will be mud, mud and more mud. Every goody-goody animal will have to leave. Hehehe!"

She disappeared in a spray of stinky sparks, her laughter echoing eerily round the trees.

Goldie's green eyes flashed with worry. "We must make sure the Bobblehops are all right," she said.

"Let's go!" cried Lily and Jess together.

 22

CHAPTER TWO

Friendship Forest in Danger!

Goldie led the way east towards the

Bobblehops' house. They had to go round

patches of squelchy mud. Timmy and

Tommy Sparklepaw were under the

Treasure Tree gathering apples. They

waved happily. But the mud had crept up

to the tree and the little white kittens kept slipping over.

The three friends came to Bluebell Brook. The clear water glinted in the sunshine and cheerful bluebells nodded on the bank.

"I'm glad Grizelda's evil spell hasn't spoilt the brook," said Jess.

Goldie ran across the gleaming white stepping stones, the girls close behind. They were horrified to see that on the other side the ground was much muddier. Hardly a blade of grass could be seen.

They arrived at a little thatched barn

sheltering under a fragrant lilac tree.
The barn had a rose-covered porch and
a stable door. The top half of the door
was open. The wonderful caramel and
marshmallow smell of sparkleberry toast
wafted out.

"Here's the Bobblehop family's home,"
said Goldie.

Polly Bobblehop

"What an adorable house!" exclaimed Lily. "But look at the poor garden."

Gungy goo was oozing round the flowerbeds. The butterpuff bushes and honeydaisies were drooping sadly.

Goldie led the way to the door.

A young wallaby with silvery-brown fur jumped out over their heads and landed on the cobbled path. She carried a little pink bag with a blue heart.

"I'm Polly Bobblehop," she

 26

squeaked, her long ears wiggling
anxiously.

"Hi, Polly," said Jess. "I'm Jess and this
is Lily – and Goldie told us that you're
the best jumper in the forest." She smiled
down at the little wallaby, who only
came up to her knees.

"I love jumping!" said Polly. "I used
to jump everywhere. I especially liked
sploshing in the mud." Her eyes filled with
tears. "Then I got stuck in the mud near
Grizelda's tower and now I'm very scared
of it."

Lily hugged Polly. "I don't blame you.

I'd be scared too," she said.

Polly gave her a wobbly smile. Then she gazed sadly at her ruined garden.

"Have you come to stop Grizelda spoiling Friendship Forest?" she asked.

"We have!" said Jess.

A grown-up wallaby wearing a flowery headscarf opened the bottom half of the door.

"I'm Mrs Bobblehop," she said in a gentle voice. "Polly's mum. Do come inside."

Polly led the girls into a cosy kitchen. Three young wallabies sat at the table,

 28

eating sparkleberry toast and drinking

frothy milk. They waved at Lily and Jess,

but the girls could see they were worried.

"These are my little brothers," said

Polly. "Monty and Max are twins, and

Noah is the baby."

Polly's dad was sweeping up glass

from a broken picture frame above the

mantelpiece. He smiled at them.

"I'm so glad you've come," he said. "We know you'll help us beat that dreadful witch."

"Tell us what happened," said Goldie.

Mr Bobblehop leaned on his broom handle. "The map was kept in this frame. We thought it was safe. We'd just sat down

to breakfast when Grizelda flew in, smashed the frame and snatched the map."

"Burrrppp!"

A strange creature was floating at the door. He was small, green and almost see-through with wide round eyes. He burped again and Monty, Max and Noah giggled.

Lily and Jess had seen creatures like him before. He was one of the wind sprites who'd worked with Grizelda when she stole the other maps.

"I'm Gust, the sprite of the east wind," announced the creature. He whirled round the girls' heads, making them feel dizzy. Then he let out another loud

31

burp and chuckled so hard his whole body quivered like jelly.

"I've hidden your measly map," he taunted. "And you'll never find it! Soon there'll only be mucky mud."

He vanished with a burp.

"If the forest gets covered in mud, we'll have to leave," said

Polly, her lip trembling.

Little Noah gave a whimper of fear.
Mrs Bobblehop tucked him into her
pouch. "We can't let Grizelda drive us
from our homes," she whispered.

"Don't worry," said Jess. "We'll find
your map."

"And the forest will be beautiful again,"
said Lily.

"I do hope so," sighed Mrs Bobblehop.
She gasped as gloopy brown mud began
to ooze over the doorstep.

"Quick, everybody," said Mr
Bobblehop. "We must go upstairs."

 33

Mrs Bobblehop hurried the twins up the steps. But Polly stayed where she was.

"Can I come with you?" she asked the three friends. "I want to help."

"But you're scared of mud, Polly," said her father.

"We must save our home – and the forest," insisted Polly, making her paws into little furry fists.

"You're very brave," said Mr Bobblehop, giving his daughter a kiss. "Promise to be careful."

"I promise," said Polly. She hurried down the path with Goldie and the girls.

Polly Bobblehop

They stopped at the gate to wave.

Polly's brothers waved back from a
bedroom window. "Good luck!" they called.

"You can count on us!" cried Lily and
Jess.

They turned towards the trees. Round
the trunks, puddles of mud were bubbling
and swirling.

"Oh dear," squeaked Polly. "I *must* be
brave."

"You can do it," said Lily. "And together
we'll save Friendship Forest."

 36

CHAPTER THREE

Swept Away!

"Where could Gust have hidden the map?" asked Polly anxiously.

"It might be anywhere," said Goldie. "In the caverns, on Magic Mountain, or even in Grizelda's tower."

"Whatever happens to the map happens to Friendship Forest," said Jess.

 37

"So if the forest is getting muddy then the map must be somewhere muddy."

"That's right, Jess!" said Lily. "Where are the muddiest places in Friendship Forest?"

"The Muddlepups' garden when the cheeky pups have a water fight!" said Goldie.

"It can get quite squishy near Sparkly Falls," added Jess.

"But the muddiest place in the whole forest is the Boggits' swamp!" exclaimed Lily.

The Boggits were ogre-like creatures who used to work for Grizelda. They loved smells and rubbish and gloopy mud. The girls and the animals had made them a mucky, rubbish-filled swamp to live in. In return the Boggits had agreed never to work for the horrible witch again, and they'd become friends with all the animals.

"Well done, Lily," declared Goldie. "Gust wouldn't even need any magic

mud – he could just drop the map in the swamp. We'll go there right away."

"Whoa!" cried Jess, grabbing hold of Lily to stop herself falling. "The ground's so gooey I can hardly walk!"

"My feet keep slipping too," said Lily.

"I'm scared I'll get stuck," said Polly anxiously.

Jess stared at the mud. Sticky blobs swelled up and burst, sending smelly green sparks splattering everywhere. "This isn't ordinary mud," she muttered.

"Grizelda's added an evil spell to it," agreed Lily.

"We need something to help us walk," said Jess. "Let's find some nice long walking sticks."

The friends all looked around.

"That's odd," said Goldie. "There are usually lots of sticks here but now I can't see a single one."

A loud burp suddenly exploded behind a nearby bush, making the leaves shake.

"That's Gust!" cried Polly.

 41

"No it isn't," Gust's voice came from behind the bush.

Lily and Jess walked round the bush and found Gust floating above a pile of sticks. They were all the right length to be walking sticks, with knobbly bits to make them easy to grip.

"You hid all the sticks!" Lily said.

"Walking sticks are a silly idea," Gust pouted.

"No, they're a good idea and

that's why you hid them," grinned Jess.

They each grabbed a stick.

Gust gave an angry burp and vanished.

Ahead they could hear gungy, gurgling

noises as a wide river came into view.

Dirty brown water rushed along in

gloopy waves. Nasty green sparks burst

up everywhere.

"I don't recognise this," said Polly.

"Where are we?"

"It's Bluebell Brook," said Goldie in

alarm. "It wasn't like this when we crossed

it earlier."

The stepping stones were now covered

in slippery slime.

"How will we get across?" cried Lily.

"I'll jump," exclaimed Polly. She sprang over the river and landed on the far bank with a big splosh. "The mud's really deep here," she called in fear. "Please hurry."

"We can't jump like Polly," Goldie told Lily and Jess. "We'll have to use the stepping stones."

She began to pick her way from stone to stone. The girls gasped as her paws

skidded but she balanced herself with a
swish of her tail. At last she reached the
other side.

"Now it's our turn," gulped Lily.

Jess stepped on to the slimy stones
and moved slowly into the middle of
the torrent. Lily followed but the mucky
water surged over her shoes and sucked
her stick away. Her feet began to slide.

Jess turned to see her friend fighting
to keep upright. She grabbed her hand.

Lily lost her footing and clutched at Jess. With a horrifying splash the two friends plunged into the river!

They felt themselves sinking in the foul water. Spluttering, they struggled to the surface and tried to swim to the bank, but the current was too strong.

"Help!" they cried.

Goldie came streaking along the bank. Polly bounded after her.

"Hold on to this!" cried Polly, holding her stick over the water.

Lily grabbed it and clung on. With a nasty crack, the stick snapped in two.

Polly didn't give up. She stretched out
her paws.

"No," called Goldie. "You'll be pulled in
too." She wrapped her tail around Polly's
feet. "Now try. I'll keep you safe."

 47

The girls reached for the wallaby's paws. Their hands were too slimy with mud. They couldn't hold on.

Jess gave a frightened cry as the churning river swept them away. "Look out! Rocks ahead!"

"We must get out of this river," gasped Lily, catching sight of the sharp, jagged shapes. "If we don't, we'll be thrown right on to them!"

CHAPTER FOUR

Mr Stoutfoot's Wonderful Boots

The river whooshed Lily and Jess along.
The rocks were getting nearer.

Jess realised she was still clutching her
stick. "Grab this!" she shouted to Lily. Lily
caught the end.

"Now kick!" cried Jess. "If we work

together we'll be stronger."

They kicked as hard as they could. Nothing happened. But they weren't going to give up. At last they began to move through the muddy water towards the bank. Goldie held out her paws and hauled them from the river.

Polly came hopping up. "You were so brave," she said. "I'd have been really scared."

Lily gave her

a warm smile. "Thank you for trying to
rescue us," she said. "I'd hug you, but I'm
too mucky!"

Gust swooped in front of them with
a noisy burp. "Mud, mud, wonderful
mud!" he sniggered when he saw the girls
dripping with slime. "Lovely day for a
swim."

The four friends ignored him and set
off towards the swamp. Polly and Lily had
lost their sticks and had to hold on to Jess
and Goldie. But their feet kept slipping
from under them.

"This is no good," said Jess. "We need

 51

something sturdy, like Wellington boots."

"I bet Billy Stoutfoot would have some," Goldie suggested.

Billy Stoutfoot the goat was the Friendship Forest cobbler.

"That's a good idea!" said Lily, "Let's go."

Just then, they heard a little voice coming from a clump of trees. "Help me, oh please help me! I'm stuck in the mud!"

"Who's there?" asked Polly, hopping towards the voice.

"It's me, Jimmy Tiddletoe. I'm a mouse and BUUUUUUUURP!"

"Hold on," said Lily. "That doesn't sound like a mouse!"

Polly pushed a branch aside and they saw Gust hovering over a thick, sticky patch of mud.

"Gust! You were tricking us!" said Lily.

"You tried to get us to rescue you so that we would get stuck in the mud, didn't you?" said Jess.

Gust gave a burp of despair and slumped in a puddle. "Stupid, clever girls," he whined.

The friends ignored the mean sprite. Polly let the branches go and they walked on.

Billy Stoutfoot's little workshop nestled into the hillside at the foot of the Heathertop Hills. They went up to the corn-coloured door, knocked and pushed it open.

They entered a cosy room with a workbench covered in scraps of silk and leather. Shelves stretched from floor to ceiling, full of brightly coloured shoes and slippers.

A golden-brown goat with curved horns and shiny green boots was sitting in the corner. It was Billy Stoutfoot. Lily and Jess were pleased to see Holly Santapaws with him. The cobbler and the little white

puppy were giggling. Billy took a sip from a small silver bottle. Then he tweeted like a bird. He suddenly spotted his visitors.

"Hello, there," he said. "Come and try Holly's new invention."

Holly Santapaws was a very clever inventor. Her Soapy Suds Cleaning Solution had once saved Christmas in Friendship Forest.

"It's called a Sweet Tweet," said Holly. She pulled out another bottle from her basket and offered it to Lily. "It makes you sing like a bird."

Lily tasted the foamy, orangey-pink

 56

drink. "*Tweet, tweet, tweet!*"

Everyone laughed.

"It tastes like peach sherbet," Lily giggled.

"I wish we could all have a go," said Goldie. "But we don't have time. We have a special favour to ask, Mr Stoutfoot."

She explained about Grizelda's evil plan.

"So that's why there's so much mud!" said Holly. "How awful."

"We need some of your wonderful boots

so we can get through it," Lily told Billy
Stoutfoot.

The goat rubbed his beard. "I've got
just the thing." He rummaged through
a cupboard and pulled out four pairs of
boots.

The friends admired the pretty wellies.
They were pink and covered in patterns
of sparkling violets and daisies. As they
slipped their feet in, the boots magically
changed so that they fitted perfectly.

"They're so comfy," said Jess, looking at
them in the cobbler's little mirror.

"Thank you, Mr Stoutfoot," said

Goldie. "We're really grateful."

"I'd do anything to help you defeat that witch," declared the cobbler.

Billy Stoutfoot and Holly waved goodbye as the four friends left the shop and headed for Boggit Swamp.

"These are lovely boots," exclaimed Polly. "I could hop for ever!"

She bounced up and down. Lily and

Jess laughed and dodged the splashes of mud she made.

Then Lily caught her paws. "Listen, Polly," she said. "We're going to the muddiest place in the forest. You don't have to come with us."

Polly stopped bouncing. "It sounds terrifying," she said in a small voice. "But I'm not going to let Grizelda win."

"You're very brave, just like your dad said," declared Jess.

"What are we waiting for?" cried Goldie. "Off to Boggit Swamp!"

CHAPTER FIVE

Boggit Swamp

The four friends strode along in their sturdy wellies.

Friendship Forest was certainly looking very sad. There wasn't a flower to be seen anywhere and mud was bubbling up the tree trunks. Anxious eyes peered out from among the leaves.

"Please help save the forest, Lily and Jess!" called Sophie and Woody Flufftail. The little squirrels were clinging to a high branch.

"We'll do our best," Jess called back.

They reached the clearing of Boggit Swamp. A thick, squelchy bog swirled around their boots.

The surface bubbled and popped, sending out smelly green sparks.

"The whole place is covered in

Grizelda's nasty mud," said Goldie.

Polly shuddered. "I hate to think of our precious map being in here."

There was a strong smell of rotten cauliflower, and four gnarly creatures lumbered out of a hut in the middle.

"Pongo and Reek!" exclaimed Jess happily.

"And Whiffy and Sniff!" added Lily with a smile.

The Boggits had big grins on their grimy faces. They waded through the swamp, waving. Mud dripped off their grubby, multi-coloured fur.

 63

"Hello!" they chorused in their gravelly voices.

"Swamp lovely today," said Pongo. "Mud really deep!"

"Whiffy like mud," said Whiffy, smothering herself in the stinky mess. "More mud good."

"This isn't good mud," said Jess. "It's horrible magic mud. Grizelda put it here."

"She's stolen the Bobblehops' map," explained Lily. She told the Boggits about Grizelda's evil plan and their search for the map. "If the mud spreads and covers all of Friendship Forest, the animals will

have to leave."

"Animals not leave!" cried Reek in alarm.

Sniff shook her head, spraying flecks of dirt everywhere. "If animals go, Sniff sad," she said.

"Boggits look for map!" declared Pongo firmly.

 65

"Thank you," said Jess. "We think it's hidden in your swamp."

Polly gave an anxious whimper. "I'm scared to go in," she said. "I might get stuck."

Lily's heart melted at the little wallaby's sad expression. "Don't worry, Polly," she said kindly. "You stay here on the bank."

The girls and Goldie waded into the swamp

and began to search. The Boggits joined in, throwing handfuls of gloop about.

After a while, Jess stopped. "Is it my imagination or is there even more mud now?" she asked.

"You're right," gasped Goldie. "It's reached the top of my boots."

"Yuck! It's dripping down inside mine," cried Lily. She tried to walk but found she couldn't. "I'm stuck!" she called in fright.

"Me too," said Jess.

"And me!" said Goldie. "Can you help us, Boggits?"

"Whiffy help!" declared Whiffy. She

swung her arms
but her feet didn't
move. "Whiffy not
help. Whiffy stuck!"

"Bad mud not
let us move!"
growled Reek.
"Swamp not nice."

"Never get out!" wailed Sniff.

Jess caught Lily's eye. If they really
were all stuck, how could they ever save
Friendship Forest?

CHAPTER SIX

Lovely Mud!

Lily held out her hands to Goldie and Jess. "Let's try to move together," she said.

But it was no good. Grizelda's mud had them trapped.

"Nasty Grizelda," muttered Pongo, thumping the sticky goo with his big fists.

"And there's no sign of the map,"

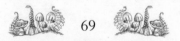

Goldie added sadly.

A soft *buuurp* sounded from behind the Boggits' ramshackle hut in the middle of the swamp.

The friends looked around.

"I wonder why Gust is hiding behind the hut?" Jess muttered.

Suddenly Lily spotted a glimmer of silver in the middle of the swamp, next to the Boggit hut.

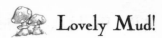

"It's because the map's right there!" she exclaimed.

A corner of the map was sticking out of the goo. But it was sinking. Soon it would be swallowed up. The girls tried to wade to it but their boots were glued to the bottom of the swamp.

Gust flew out from behind the hut, looking panicked. "You stay away from that map!" He started blowing at them,

making a strong wind that blew their hair
and fur right back.

"Stop it, Gust!"
said Jess.

"*BUUURP!*" said
Gust. "Oh, these
silly burps! I've led
you right to the
map with them.
Grizelda's going to
be so cross with me!" He zoomed away,
huffing to himself.

"What are we going to do?" asked Lily
in alarm. "The swamp's rising so fast!"

 72

"I'll get the map," declared Polly.

"Are you sure, Polly?" asked Goldie. "You might get stuck like us."

Polly trembled a little, but she gave a determined nod. "My back legs are strong so I won't get stuck like you. It's our only way to save Friendship Forest," she said with a gulp.

The map had almost disappeared.

"Map going down!" warned Whiffy.

Polly hopped back a few paces, bounded forwards and took an enormous leap, soaring high into the air. She landed with a huge, slurpy splash in the middle of the swamp. She reached for the map but it slipped from her muddy paws. Frowning hard in concentration, she tried again but this time the map disappeared under the surface! Polly plunged her paws deep into the mud. Lily and Jess held their breath. It felt like hours before they saw a glimmer of silver. At last Polly held the map up in triumph.

"You did it!" cried Lily, Jess and Goldie.

"Boggits happy!" shouted Pongo.

Polly was beaming. "That wasn't as scary as I thought it would be!" she declared. "And look! I'm not stuck."

74

She began to hop around, her back legs pushing her clear of the mud.

"You're such a strong jumper that you're not getting stuck!" cried Lily.

"Well done, Polly," shouted Jess.

"I can rescue you now!" Polly called, her eyes shining with happiness.

 75

Polly bounded up to Lily, Jess and Goldie. She pulled each one out of the mud in turn. Then she freed the Boggits. As they stood on the bank, Jess gave Polly a kiss on her soft cheek.

"You've saved Friendship Forest," she said.

"Polly brave!" shouted the Boggits. "Polly clever."

"Thank you," said Polly happily.

Goldie still looked worried.

"What's wrong?" asked Jess.

"There's something we didn't think of," said Goldie, desperately trying to wipe off the brown goo that hung in big sticky blobs from the map. "Friendship Forest won't be free of mud until the map is clean. And I can't get the mud off!"

The smiles turned to anxious frowns.

"If we can't find a way to clean it ... " began Polly.

Goldie's green eyes filled with tears. "... then Friendship Forest is doomed," she whispered.

CHAPTER SEVEN

Bubbles and Burps!

"There must be a way to clean the map!" declared Polly, thumping her tail on the ground.

Everybody thought hard.

"Surely there's someone who can help us," said Lily. "After all, Mr Stoutfoot gave us these wonderful boots, the Boggits looked for the map with us …"

"Holly Santapaws!" cried Lily. Her
friends looked at her in surprise. "Do you
remember the adventure we had with
her? We used her Soapy Suds Cleaning
Solution, and it cleans anything."

Jess gave Lily
a muddy hug.
"That's so clever,"
she said. "Let's find
Holly."

"She might
still be with Mr
Stoutfoot!" said

Polly, bounding ahead.

Shouting goodbye to the Boggits, Lily, Jess and Goldie hurried after the eager little wallaby. Fighting against the deep, gloopy slime, they arrived at last at the cobbler's shop. They pushed the door open … and there was Holly, saying goodbye to Billy Stoutfoot.

"We're so glad we've caught you, Holly!" panted Jess.

The white puppy wagged her tail in excitement as she spotted the map in Goldie's paws. "You've found it!" she gasped. "Now everything will be fine."

81

"Only if we can get this gunge off it," explained Lily. "Please may we have some of your wonderful cleaning solution?"

"You're in luck," said Holly, taking a small jar from her basket. "I've got some here." She looked outside. Waves of brown goo were sloshing up the path to the workshop.

"Pour it on!" urged Polly. "Quickly!"

"I must mix it with water first," said Holly. Billy Stoutfoot filled a bowl from the tap. Holly poured the mixture into it. The water swirled about, making beautiful colours. Then it grew still.

 82

Goldie placed the map in the bowl.

Lily grabbed Jess's hand. They knew
they were both thinking the same thing.
What if the cleaning solution didn't work?

A big blue bubble formed in the bowl,
on the surface of the water. *Pop!* The
bubble burst. In a trice the mud vanished
and the Bobblehops' map was as good as

new. Each path, tree and stream on the silver parchment was sparkly clean!

At once there was a gurgly, slurping sound, like water going down a giant plughole. Grizelda's evil mud began to disappear.

"Hurrah!" cried Jess.

Lily and Polly danced round in delight. But they soon stopped. Every step was sending up a huge splash of water.

"The ground's still horribly damp and squelchy," said Lily.

Goldie held up the map. "That's because the map is still soaking wet,"

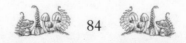

she said. She flapped it backwards and
forwards to dry the parchment. "Oh dear.
It's just as soggy."

She dabbed it
with her scarf but
it didn't help.

"And, oh no!"
said Goldie.
"The wetness is
making the ink on the map run!"

They heard a sound in a nearby bush
and a nose poked out through the leaves.
"Hehehe," came a giggle. "The mud's
gone. But if the ink runs, the forest will be

ruined anyway. *Burrpp!*"

Polly looked out of the window. "The trees look strange. As if they're stretching and fading."

"Like the ink on the page!" said Lily.

Gust laughed and twirled with glee.

"We need to get this map dry quickly!" said Goldie.

Gust burped and giggled.

"I wish Gust would leave us alone," said Jess crossly. "I can't think with him here."

Lily's eyes lit up. "No, Gust is just who we need." The others looked at her in astonishment. "He's a wind sprite. If we

ask

nicely

maybe he'll blow

the map dry!"

"Never!" Gust called

from his bush.

"Please, Gust," called

Polly. "You could do it so

easily."

"No!" insisted Gust. "Grizelda won't

like that! *Burrpp!* Oh, these annoying

burps!"

"I have a plan," Lily whispered to the

others. She turned to the bush. "We have

87

a lovely drink that will stop your burps, Gust. Look."

She pulled out the Sweet Tweets bottle, took a sip and a beautiful burst of birdsong flew out of her mouth.

Gust whooshed out from the bush. His eyes were sparkling. "That sounds nice!" he cried. "I want some."

"Of course," said Lily, "as long as you dry our map first."

"Shan't!" declared Gust. He looked pleadingly at the bottle. The girls held their breath. "All right," he said at last. "I'll do it."

He filled his cheeks with air and blew
with all his might at the map. Polly gave
a squeal as a strong wind began to blast
round the trees.

"Don't worry, Polly," Jess assured her.
"The wind is only blowing in the forest
because Gust is blowing on the map."

Leaves and twigs were tossed into the air and Goldie's scarf was flapping wildly as she tried to stand up against the gale.

At last Gust stopped.

"The map's dry!" declared Goldie.

Lily felt the grass. "This is dry too," she exclaimed.

"And the ink has stopped running," said Jess, smiling.

Polly hopped up and down. "There's not a splash or a splosh left," she squealed happily.

"The animals' homes have been saved!" said Goldie.

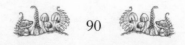

"Thank you, Gust," said Jess. "That was brilliant." She gave the Sweet Tweets bottle to the wind sprite.

"Here goes!" he shouted, and took a gulp. He opened his mouth and began to tweet a jolly melody. "This is much nicer than burping!" he said, when the song came to an end. "I'm glad I helped you."

"Our forest is saved!" cried Goldie. "We must celebrate."

"Can I join in?" asked Gust anxiously.

"Of course you can," said Lily.

Gust rushed around their heads in an excited whirlwind.

 91

"Everyone to my house," said Polly. "It's party time!"

CHAPTER EIGHT

Party at the Bobblehops'

The Bobblehops' garden was full of happy

partygoers. Mr Bobblehop had fixed the

silver map in a brand-new frame and it

was back over the mantelpiece where it

belonged.

The Longwhiskers family arrived

with baskets of food from the Toadstool

 93

Café. Olivia Nibblesqueak had baked a huge, gooey mud pie especially for the celebration.

"It looks like mud," she giggled, "but it's really chocolate."

Gust whizzed about, swigging the Sweet Tweets drink and tweeting party songs.

"I'm a bit muddy for a party," laughed Jess. She looked round. Everyone had dirty feet and splashes of slime on their clothes.

"I'll clean everybody up!" announced Holly Santapaws. She mixed up her

Soapy Suds Cleaning Solution and made

giant rainbow bubbles. It was such fun

to run in and out of the fizzy suds. Soon

there wasn't a trace of mud on anyone.

"That's a strange bubble," said Polly,

pointing at a yellowish-green orb

whizzing towards the party.

"It's not a bubble," exclaimed Lily in

horror.

The orb burst

in a shower of

stinking sparks.

Everyone gasped

as Grizelda

appeared. She

stamped her

spiked boot with

fury.

"Where's all my

marvellous mud gone?" she screeched.

The woodland creatures huddled
together in fear. Gust quivered nervously
above them.

Lily and Jess stepped boldly up to the
witch.

"We found the Bobblehops' map," Jess
told her.

"And we washed it," added Lily. "That's
why the forest is clean again."

Grizelda pointed a bony finger at the
two friends but they didn't flinch from her
evil stare. "I warned you not to meddle in
my plans," she snapped.

Polly took a big jump and landed
between them. She put her
chin in the air. "Go
away, Grizelda," she
cried.

"You might think
you've won, but I'll
be back!" spat
Grizelda,
waving her
arms. "And
next time I'll drive all the silly, simpering
animals out of Friendship Forest for
good!" She whirled around to glare at

Gust, who turned pale with fright. "This
is your fault, you useless bag of wind,"
she snarled. "Get in the bottle." She pulled
out the round bottle with the other wind
sprites in and held it open.

"You don't have to, Gust," said Jess.

Gust looked longingly at the party, but
then sighed. "I can't leave my brothers.
Thank you for the party." He whizzed
towards the bottle and was sucked in.

Grizelda rammed the stopper in and
vanished in a cloud of smelly sparks.

"Poor Gust," said Goldie. "We must try
and help those wind sprites if we can."

"When we come back, we will," said Lily. "I think we should leave you to your party now."

"Yes, we've got some more cleaning to do at home," said Jess, remembering Pixie and the cake mixture.

"Oh, then you must take some of this." Holly pressed a bottle of Soapy Suds cleaning solution into her hands.

"We're so grateful," said Mrs Bobblehop as everyone gathered to wave goodbye to the girls. "Because of you, our homes are safe again."

"We're really proud of you, Polly," said

Lily. "And we're glad you're not scared of mud any more."

"Me too!" squeaked the little wallaby, beaming from ear to ear.

The girls flung their arms round her and gave her a big hug.

Lily and Jess set off through the forest

with Goldie. The last of the light touched the trees and bushes, making them glow. Flowers poking up through the green grass began to close their petals for the night.

"Thank you for helping us get rid of Grizelda's horrible mud," said Goldie as they reached the Friendship Tree.

"We made a good team," said Jess, "along with a brave young wallaby."

They hugged goodbye and Lily and Jess soon found themselves back in Brightley Meadow.

"Time to clean Pixie up," cried Lily.

"Race you back to the house!"

Back at Jess's cottage they found Pixie just as they'd left her, covered in gooey cake mixture.

Jess scooped Pixie up and took her into the bathroom. She turned on the bath taps and poured the Soapy Suds Cleaning Solution in.

Soon the bath was filled with beautiful bubbles. They floated through the air and settled on the kitten. When they popped, her fur was fluffy and clean again. Pixie jumped from Jess's arms and leapt around the bathroom, trying to catch the bubbles.

"It's perfect!" said Lily. "A cat bath that doesn't get her wet."

"Polly Bobblehop found out that getting muddy can be fun," laughed Jess. "And Pixie's found out that getting clean can be fun, too!"

The End

Horrible Grizelda has stolen the enchanted map of Friendship Forest, and is slowly turning everything dark and witchy.

Can scrumptious kitten Imogen Scribblewhiskers help the girls draw up a plan to save the day?

Find out in the next Magic Animal Friends book,

Imogen Scribblewhiskers' Perfect Picture

Turn over for a sneak peek ...

It was a sunny spring day and Lily Hart was sitting outside Helping Paw Wildlife Hospital with her best friend, Jess Forester. Two fluffy fox cubs were playing tug-of-war with a red chewy bone. The cubs were orphans, and were being cared for at Helping Paw until they were old enough to return to the wild.

"They're so funny," Lily giggled, as one of the cubs dropped the bone and whirled around, chasing his bushy tail.

"Cute, too!" said Jess. "And they're growing fast."

Lily's parents ran the hospital from a

barn at the bottom of their garden. They looked after all sorts of sick and injured animals. Jess and Lily loved helping to care for them.

The second fox cub batted the bone into Lily's mum's vegetable garden, where it disappeared among the broccoli plants. Jess jumped up to fetch it, but a golden paw batted the bone back.

She gasped in delight. "Goldie!"

A beautiful green-eyed cat with glossy golden fur emerged from the rows of vegetables. Goldie had shown the girls the way to a secret world called Friendship

Forest. It was a magical place where the animals lived in little cottages and dens, went to school, and drank blackberry fizz in the Toadstool Café. Best of all, the animals could talk!

When Goldie reached the girls, they kneeled to stroke her golden head. She leaned against them, purring.

"It's lovely to see you," Jess said.

Goldie mewed, then darted towards Brightley Stream at the bottom of the garden.

"Let's go!" cried Lily. "Goldie's taking us on another adventure in Friendship

Forest!"

The girls ran after their friend. No time passed when they were in Friendship Forest, so they knew their parents wouldn't be worried. Goldie skipped over the stepping stones that crossed the stream, Lily and Jess skipping after her, into Brightley Meadow.

Read

Imogen Scribblewhiskers' Perfect Picture

to find out what happens next!

Magic
Animal Friends

Can Jess and Lily save the magic of
Friendship Forest from Grizelda?
Read all of series eight to find out!

COMING SOON!
Look out for
Jess and Lily's
next adventure:
Bertie Bigroar Finds His Voice!

3 stories in 1!

If you like
Magic Animal Friends,
you'll love...

Welcome to Animal Ark!

Animal-mad Amelia is sad
about moving house, until she discovers
Animal Ark, where vets look after all
kinds of animals in need.

*Join Amelia and her friend Sam for a
brand-new series of animal adventures!*

Can you keep the secret?

There's lots of fun for everyone at
www.magicanimalfriends.com

Play games and explore the secret world of
Friendship Forest, where animals can talk!

Join the
Magic Animal Friends Club!

⇥✕ Special competitions ⇥✕

⇥✕ Exclusive content ⇥✕

⇥✕ All the latest Magic Animal Friends news! ⇥✕

To join the Club, simply go to

www.magicanimalfriends.com/join-our-club/